WRITTEN BY

JANET STEVENS and SUSAN STEVENS CRUMMEL

ILLUSTRATED BY JANET STEVENS

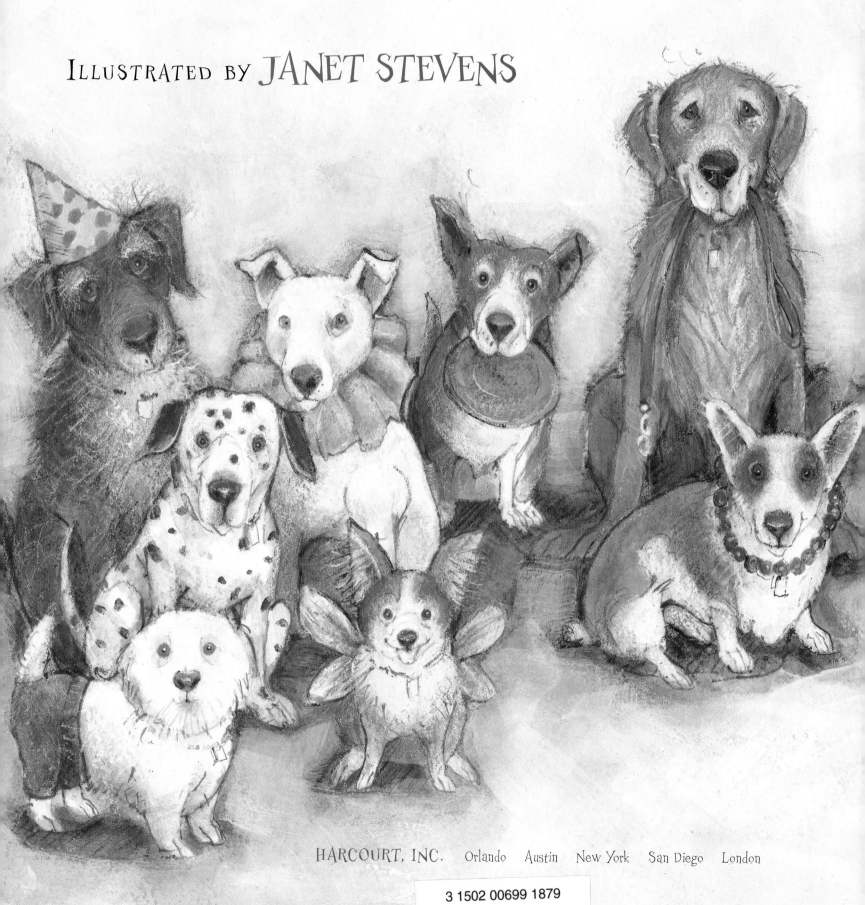

HARCOURT, INC.   Orlando   Austin   New York   San Diego   London

# Help Me, MR. MUTT!

Expert Answers for Dogs with People Problems

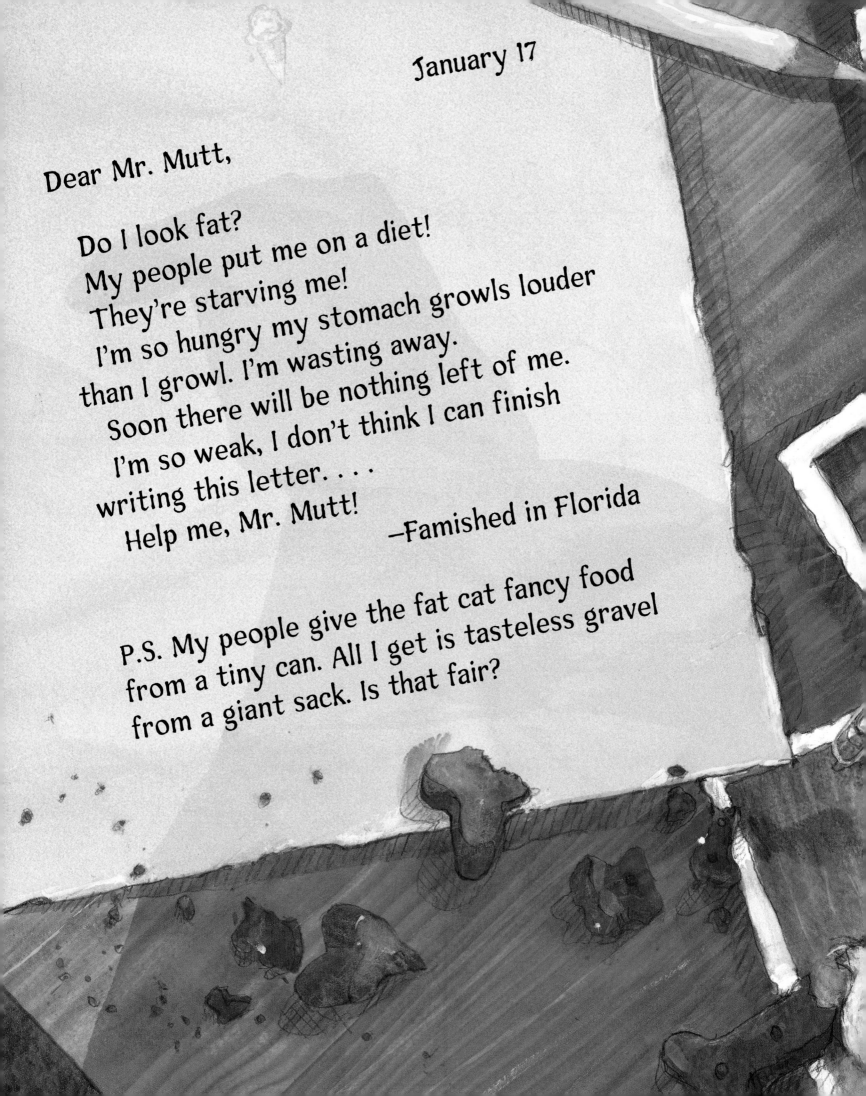

January 17

Dear Mr. Mutt,

Do I look fat?
My people put me on a diet!
They're starving me!
I'm so hungry my stomach growls louder
than I growl. I'm wasting away.
Soon there will be nothing left of me.
I'm so weak, I don't think I can finish
writing this letter. . . .
Help me, Mr. Mutt!

—Famished in Florida

P.S. My people give the fat cat fancy food
from a tiny can. All I get is tasteless gravel
from a giant sack. Is that fair?

**Mr. Mutt, Canine Counselor**
100 Bonaparte Blvd.
Dogwood, DE 19091

January 22

81 Canine Court
Dogtona Beach, FL 33133

Dear Famished,

Pull yourself together. You do not look fat. Your tummy isn't even dragging on the ground!

Study the food pyramid. Dogs require at least eight servings per day of scrumptious food. Your people do not understand this, so you have to take matters into your own paws.

← dry dog food: AVOID!

← 2 per day

← 4 per day

← 8 per day

Nice!

Look on the countertops.

Big dogs, this is easy.

Small dogs, use teamwork.

Don't forget the trash.
Be sure to dump it
out and spread it
around for the best
selection.

Little guy on the TOP!

If there's a baby
in the house, head
for the high chair
and open wide. It's
raining food!

And don't forget cleanup time. People call it kisses. We call it dessert.

Finish off your gourmet meal with a cool drink of water.

Good luck, Famished.
And remember, you are TOP DOG!

Sincerely,
Mr. Mutt

P.S. Cats are spoiled rotten. It's never fair.

The Queen

The Queen Speaks

Watch it, Muttface.
Cats are not spoiled rotten.
Especially me.
I am royalty.
I am The Queen.

P.S. The Queen would never
drink from a toilet.

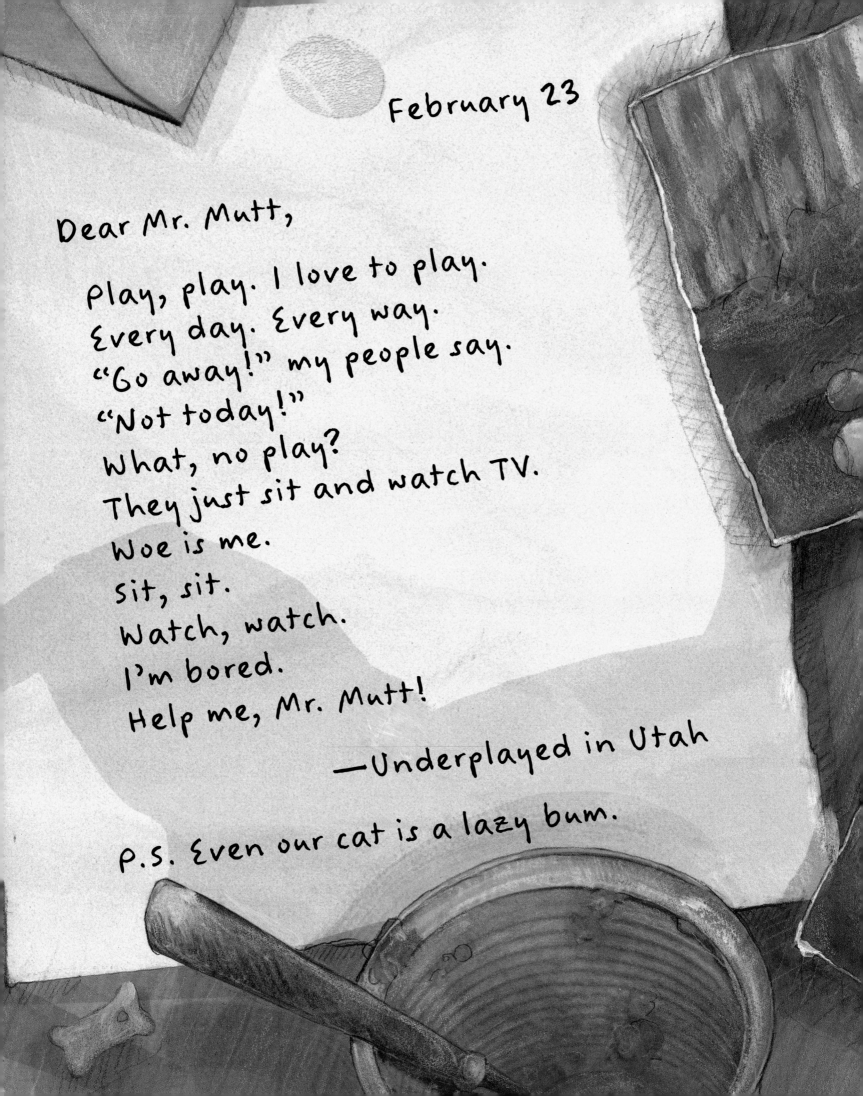

February 23

Dear Mr. Mutt,

Play, play. I love to play.
Every day. Every way.
"Go away!" my people say.
"Not today!"
What, no play?
They just sit and watch TV.
Woe is me.
Sit, sit.
Watch, watch.
I'm bored.
Help me, Mr. Mutt!

—Underplayed in Utah

P.S. Even our cat is a lazy bum.

**Mr. Mutt, Canine Counselor**
100 Bonaparte Blvd.
Dogwood, DE 19091

March 3

64 Hound Hwy.
Salty Dog City, UT 84248

Dear Underplayed,

I feel your pain. People used to play with their dogs all the time.

Then came the crash: TELEVISION. Everything changed.

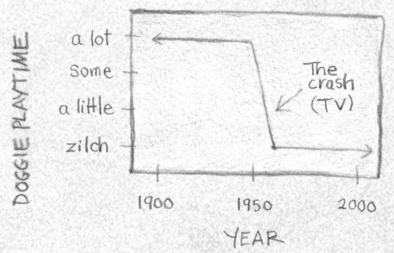

Try this. First pull the plug on that TV. Then chew the cord in two. Those couch potatoes will be bored just like you.

Now's your chance.
Get their attention.
Jump up and down.
Those potatoes will
roll off that couch
and out the door,
ready to play catch
with you!

Remind your people:
This is fun play.

←Good

Another reminder:

This is **not**
fun play!

ouch

Good luck, Underplayed.
And remember, you are TOP DOG!

Sincerely,
Mr. Mutt

P.S. If you're bored, you can always play
Chase the Cat.

GO CAT GO!

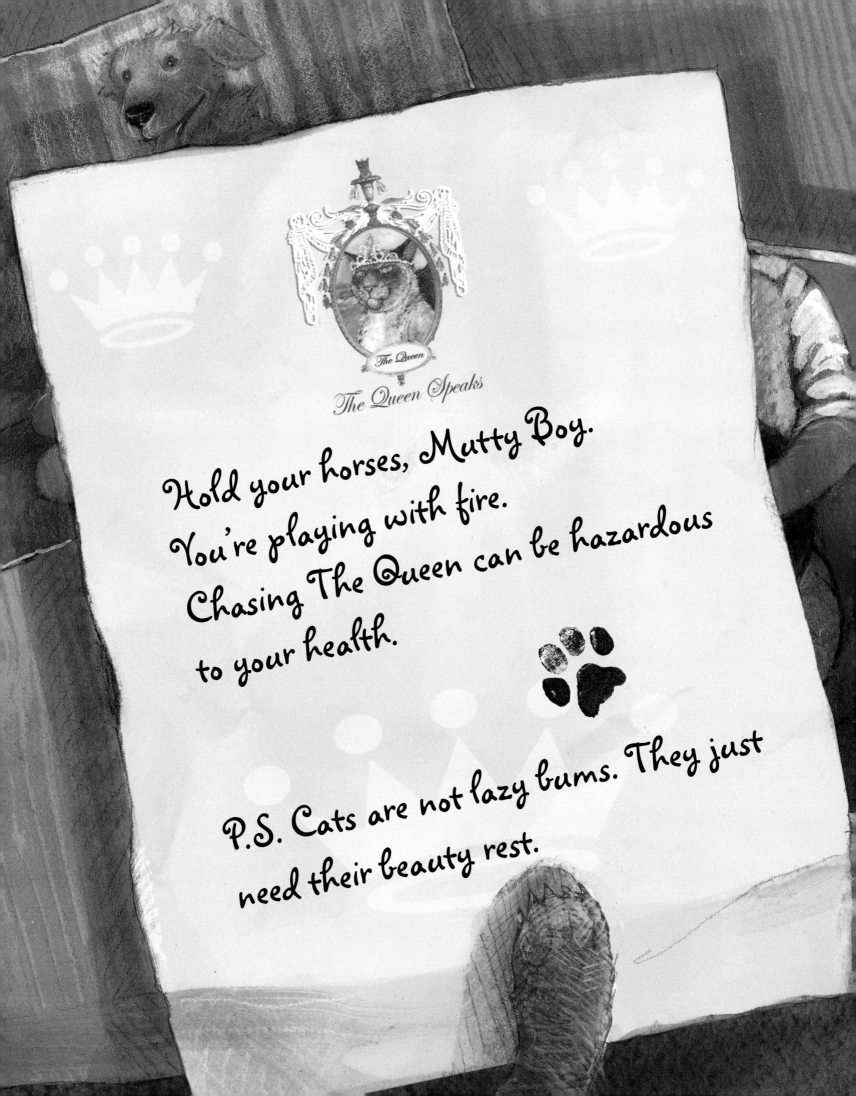

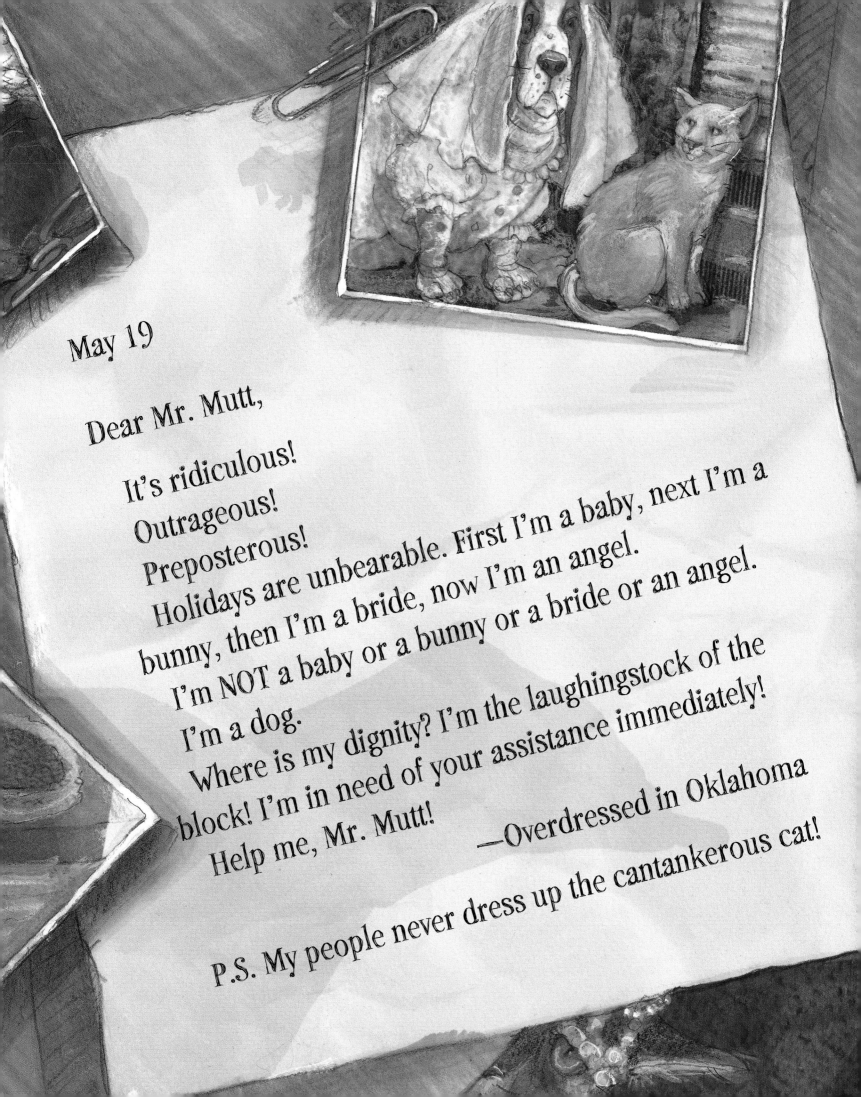

May 19

Dear Mr. Mutt,

It's ridiculous!
Outrageous!
Preposterous!
Holidays are unbearable. First I'm a baby, next I'm a bunny, then I'm a bride, now I'm an angel. I'm NOT a baby or a bunny or a bride or an angel. I'm a dog.
Where is my dignity? I'm the laughingstock of the block! I'm in need of your assistance immediately! Help me, Mr. Mutt!

—Overdressed in Oklahoma

P.S. My people never dress up the cantankerous cat!

**Mr. Mutt, Canine Counselor**
100 Bonaparte Blvd.
Dogwood, DE 19091

May 25

49 Ruff Road
Dogville, OK 73337

Dear Overdressed,

As this bar graph shows, dogs of all kinds are subjected to this foolishness, some more than others.

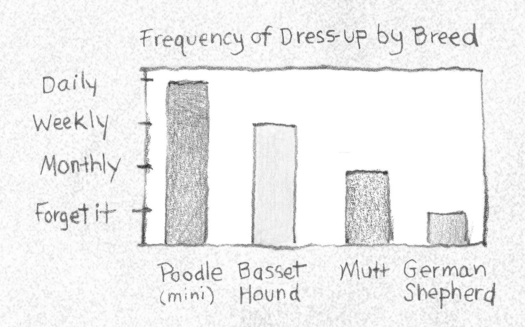

Frequency of Dress-up by Breed

In my expert opinion, you have three choices (two bad, one good):

1. <u>Rip and Run</u>. Rip off the costume and run for your life. Consequence: Your people will be mad—and you'll be in the doghouse.

2. <u>Play Dead</u>. Consequence: Your people will be worried—and you'll be at the vet.

yum
↓

3. <u>Grin and Bear it</u>. Smile and wear it. Consequence: Your people will think you're adorable—even when you're gobbling the turkey.

The choice is up to you.

Good luck, Overdressed.
And remember, you are TOP DOG!

Sincerely,
Mr. Mutt

P.S. How about this
for a kitty costume?
Don't let the cat out
of the bag!

Let me out of here!

**The Queen Speaks**

Back off, Muttbreath.
No one puts a bag on The Queen.
The Queen wears only a tiara.
Sometimes.
When she feels like it.

P.S. Cats are not cantankerous.
Cats are the sweet and gentle
supreme rulers of the universe.

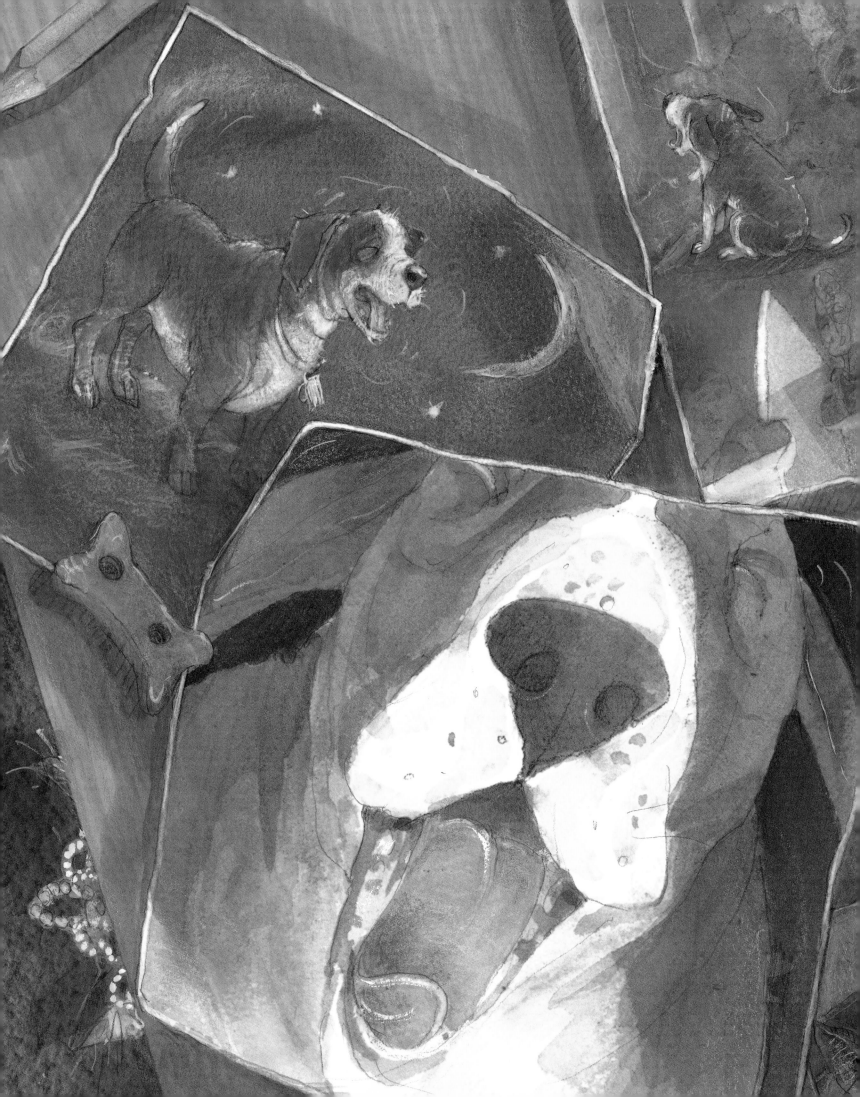

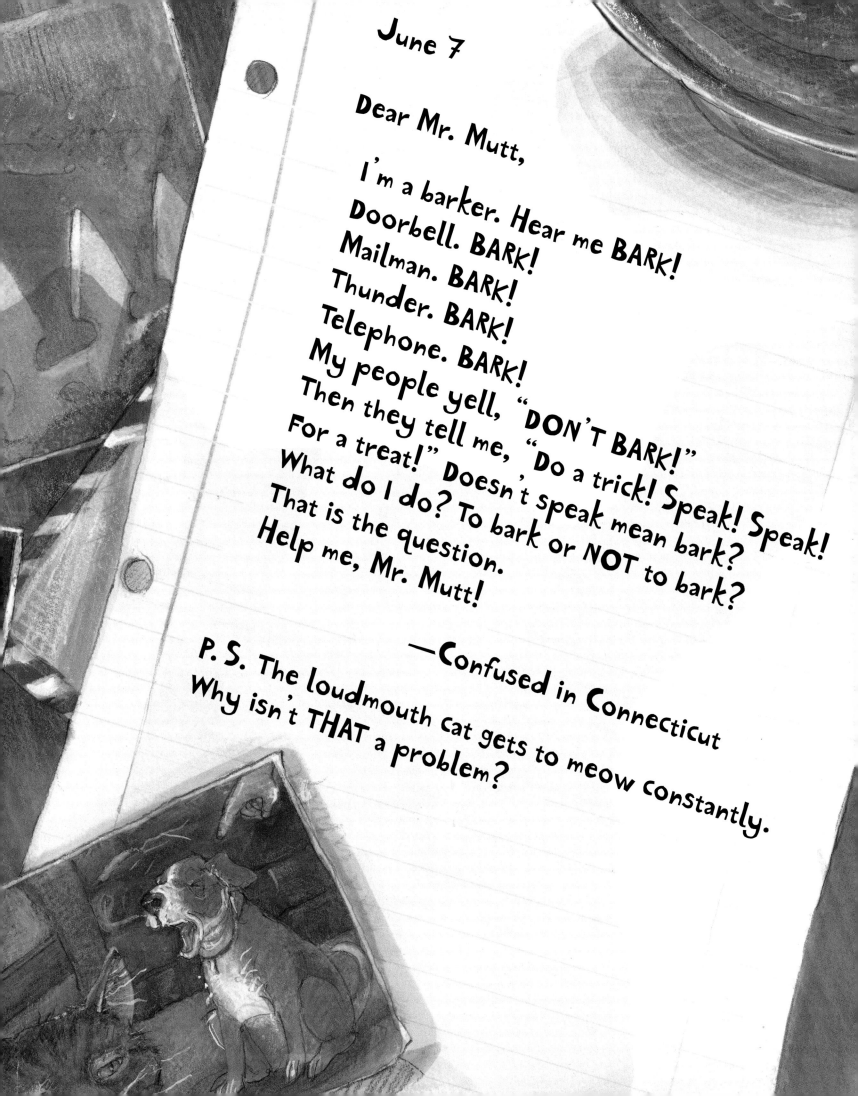

June 7

Dear Mr. Mutt,

I'm a barker. Hear me BARK!
Doorbell. BARK!
Mailman. BARK!
Thunder. BARK!
Telephone. BARK!
My people yell, "DON'T BARK!"
Then they tell me, "Do a trick! Speak! Speak! Speak!
For a treat!" Doesn't speak mean bark?
What do I do? To bark or NOT to bark?
That is the question.
Help me, Mr. Mutt!

—Confused in Connecticut

P.S. The loudmouth cat gets to meow constantly.
Why isn't THAT a problem?

**Mr. Mutt, Canine Counselor**
100 Bonaparte Blvd.
Dogwood, DE 19091

June 14

36 Speakeasy Street
Dog Haven, CT 06460

Dear Confused,

Hee-Haw!

Dogs bark. It's a fact.
It's the way we communicate.
Would people tell a duck not to quack? A cow
not to moo? A donkey not to hee-haw?

So why do your people say "Don't bark!" and
then say "Speak!"? <u>They</u> are confused, not
you!

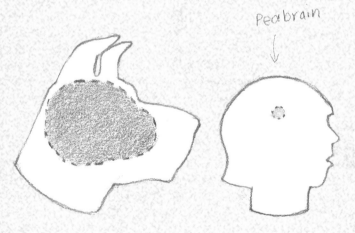

Peabrain

It's a brain thing.
The dog brain is
enormous. The people
brain is the size of
a pea. That's why
it's so easy to fool
people.

Have some fun. The next time your people say "Speak!" look them in the eye and let out a big "MOOOOO." They will be so surprised that they will drop the box of treats. It's all yours! Grab it and run.

Seriously, it's a dog-eat-treat world. Bark when you're told to. Do the tricks to get the treats. Follow this guide:

Number of treats per trick

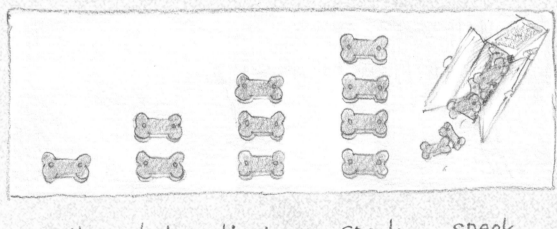

sit     shake     lie down     speak (BARK)     speak (MOO)

And if you feel the urge for some recreational barking, choose your time wisely. Wait until your people leave, then let it rip. Soon every dog in town will be barking up a storm.

Good luck, Confused.
And remember, you are TOP DOG!

Sincerely,
Mr. Mutt

P.S. You can make up some new tricks on your own, like this one: DUNK.

In you go!

The Queen

*The Queen Speaks*

You're all wet, Mutt Brain.
Don't even think of dunking
The Queen!

P.S. A meow is like music to the
ears. A lullaby. A symphony.

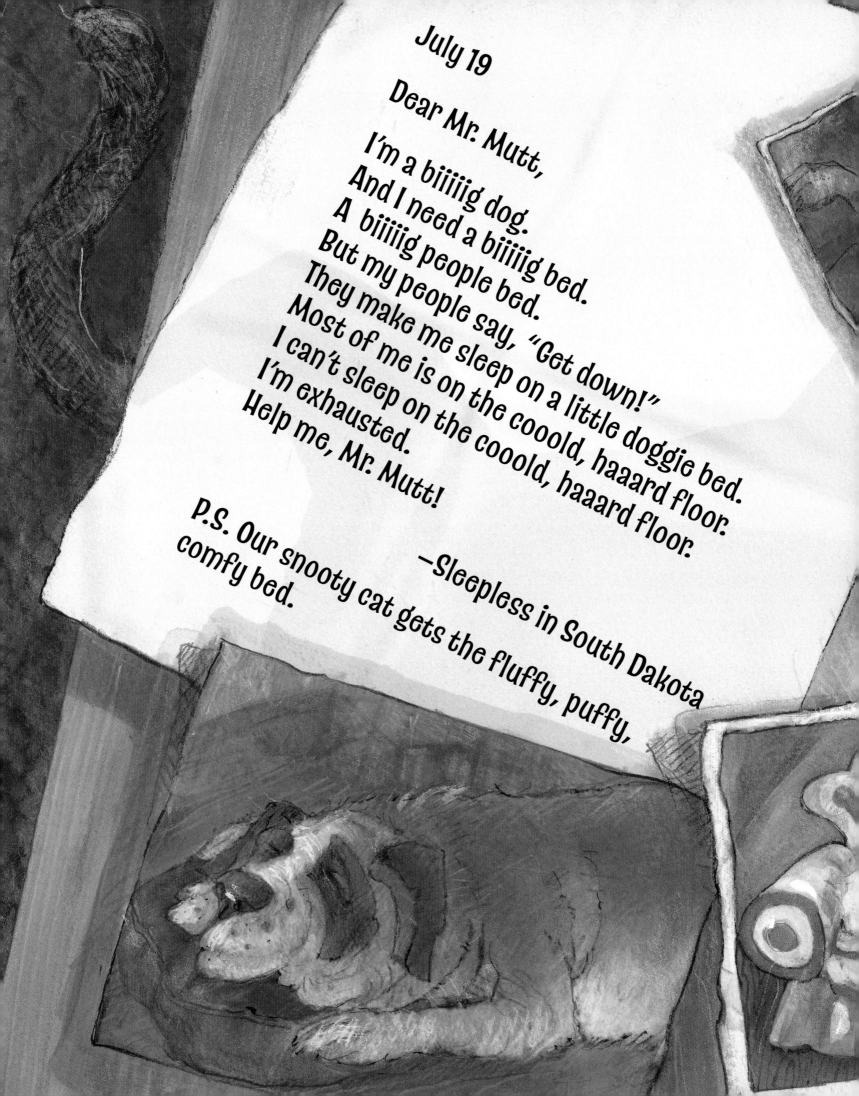

July 19

Dear Mr. Mutt,

I'm a biiiiig dog.
And I need a biiiiig bed.
A biiiiig people bed.
But my people say, "Get down!"
They make me sleep on a little doggie bed.
Most of me is on the cooold, haaard floor.
I can't sleep on the cooold, haaard floor.
I'm exhausted.
Help me, Mr. Mutt!

—Sleepless in South Dakota

P.S. Our snooty cat gets the fluffy, puffy, comfy bed.

**Mr. Mutt, Canine Counselor**
100 Bonaparte Blvd.
Dogwood, DE 19091

July 26

25 Lazy Dog Lane
Doggie Doo Falls, SD 57575

Dear Sleepless,

You are not alone. In a recent poll, nine out of ten dogs said that they definitely prefer to sleep on the people bed.

Where Sleeping Dogs Want to Lie

| | |
|---|---|
| Cold, hard floor | 0 |
| Doggie Bed | I |
| People Bed | ~~IIII~~ IIII |

Here's how you do it:

1. <u>Choose the right bed.</u>
   Grown-up bed? Too crowded.
   Baby bed? Too small.
   Kid bed? Just right.

2. <u>Choose the
   right time.</u>
   Nose on bed.
   Asleep? Check.

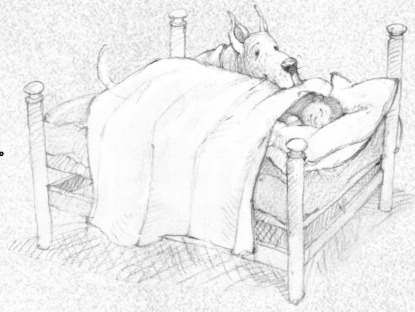

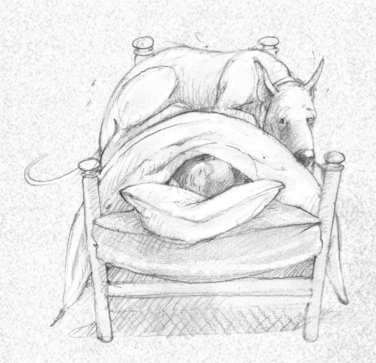

Crawl up.
Asleep? Check.

Wiggle forward. Plop!
The kid's on the floor.
Bingo! The bed is yours.

Good luck, Sleepless.
And remember, you are TOP DOG!

Sincerely,
Mr. Mutt

P.S. Use the fluffy,
puffy, comfy cat
bed for a pillow.
Better yet, use the
flea-bitten cat for
a pillow!

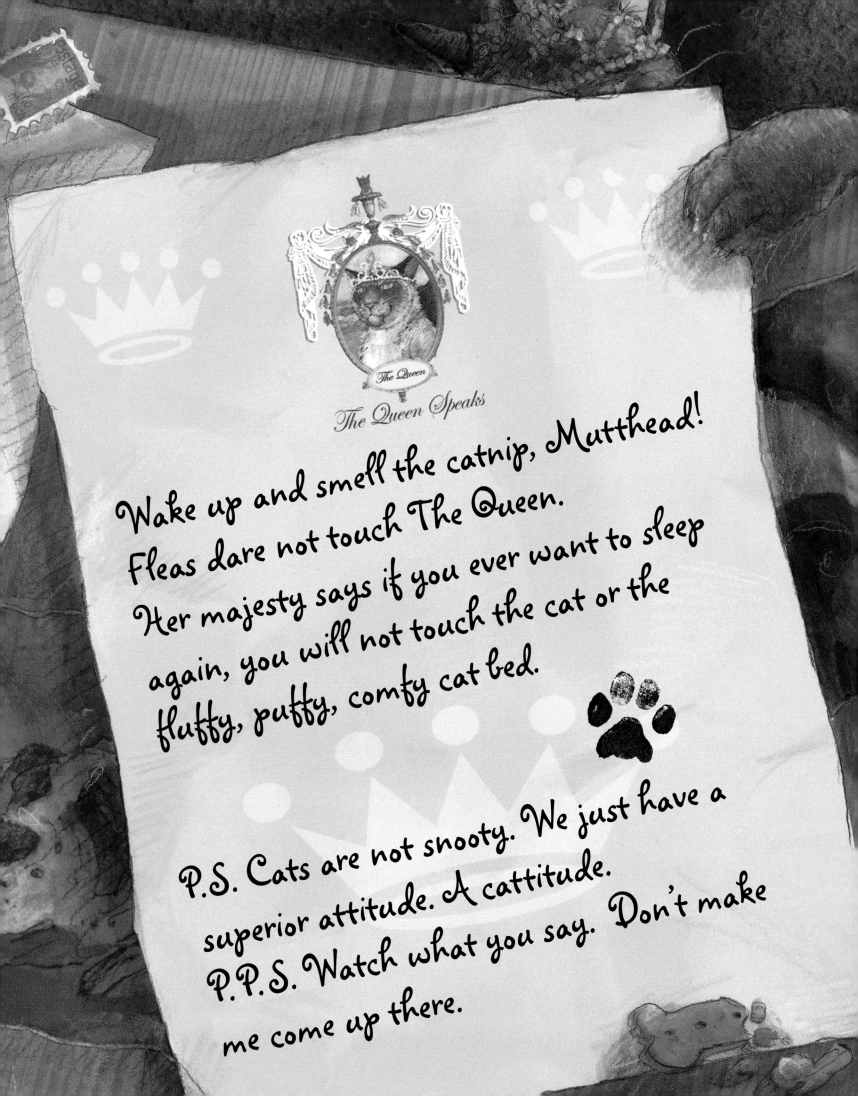

**The Queen**

*The Queen Speaks*

Wake up and smell the catnip, Mutthead! Fleas dare not touch The Queen. Her majesty says if you ever want to sleep again, you will not touch the cat or the fluffy, puffy, comfy cat bed.

P.S. Cats are not snooty. We just have a superior attitude. A cattitude.

P.P.S. Watch what you say. Don't make me come up there.

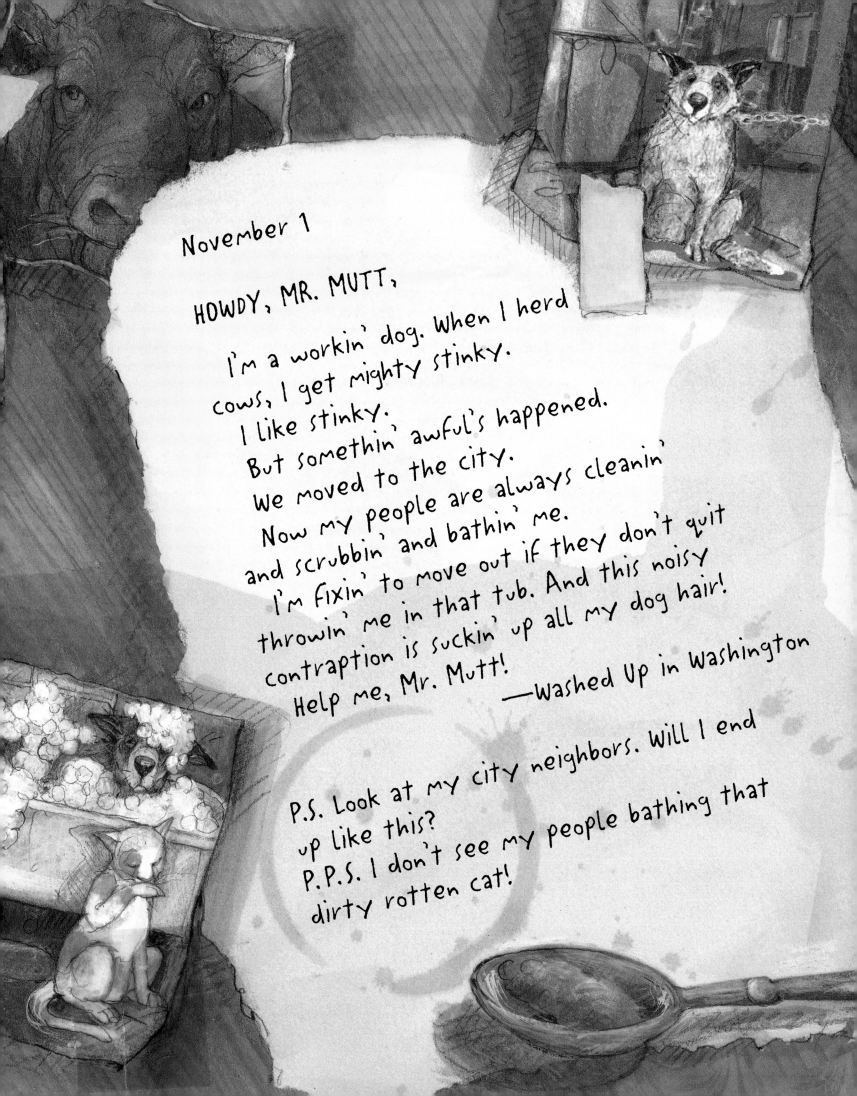

November 1

HOWDY, MR. MUTT,

I'm a workin' dog. When I herd
cows, I get mighty stinky.
I like stinky.
But somethin' awful's happened.
We moved to the city.
Now my people are always cleanin'
and scrubbin' and bathin' me.
I'm fixin' to move out if they don't quit
throwin' me in that tub. And this noisy
contraption is suckin' up all my dog hair!
Help me, Mr. Mutt!

—Washed Up in Washington

P.S. Look at my city neighbors. Will I end
up like this?
P.P.S. I don't see my people bathing that
dirty rotten cat!

**Mr. Mutt, Canine Counselor**
100 Bonaparte Blvd.
Dogwood, DE 19091

November 7

16 Prissy Pooch Parkway
Woof Woof, WA 98689

Dear Washed Up,

City folks are all clean
freaks. Neatniks.
Tidy-uppers. They could
scrub the spots off
a Dalmatian!

LOOK!

If you don't want to end up like your
neighbors, you have to put your paw down
right now! Get your smell back. Work up
a stink.

If your people get you in the tub, start shaking. They will take off running. Jump out and follow. Shake, shake. Down the hall. Shake, shake, shake. On the bed. Shake it up, baby.

This will reduce your tub time to the proper amount.

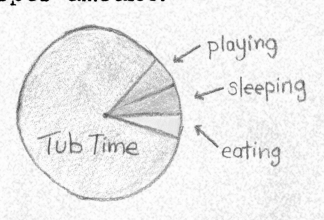

BEFORE

AFTER

Good luck, Washed Up.
And remember, you are TOP DOG!

Sincerely,
Mr. Mutt

P.S. I don't know why people
hate dog hair. I'm covered
with it and I like it!
People should use that noisy
contraption to suck up
cat hair—while it's
still on the dirty
rotten cat!

CAT

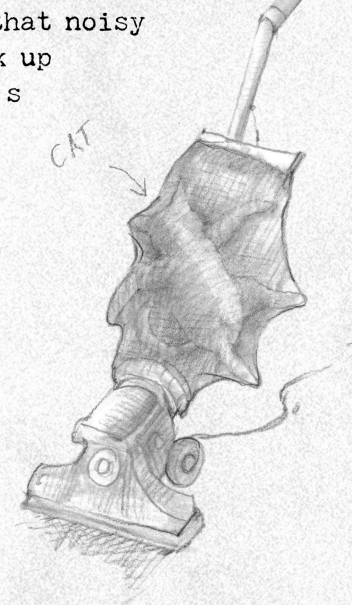

The Queen

**The Queen Speaks**

Are you nutso, Muttso?
I've had enough of your catty remarks.
Not another peep out of you.
The Queen is taking control.
You are officially out of business!

# ATTENTION ALL DOGS!

Mr. Mutt is tied up right now.
He can't help you and you can't help him.
THE QUEEN HAS TAKEN OVER.

The Queen

You got a problem?
You're a dog.
That's your problem.

Solve it yourself.

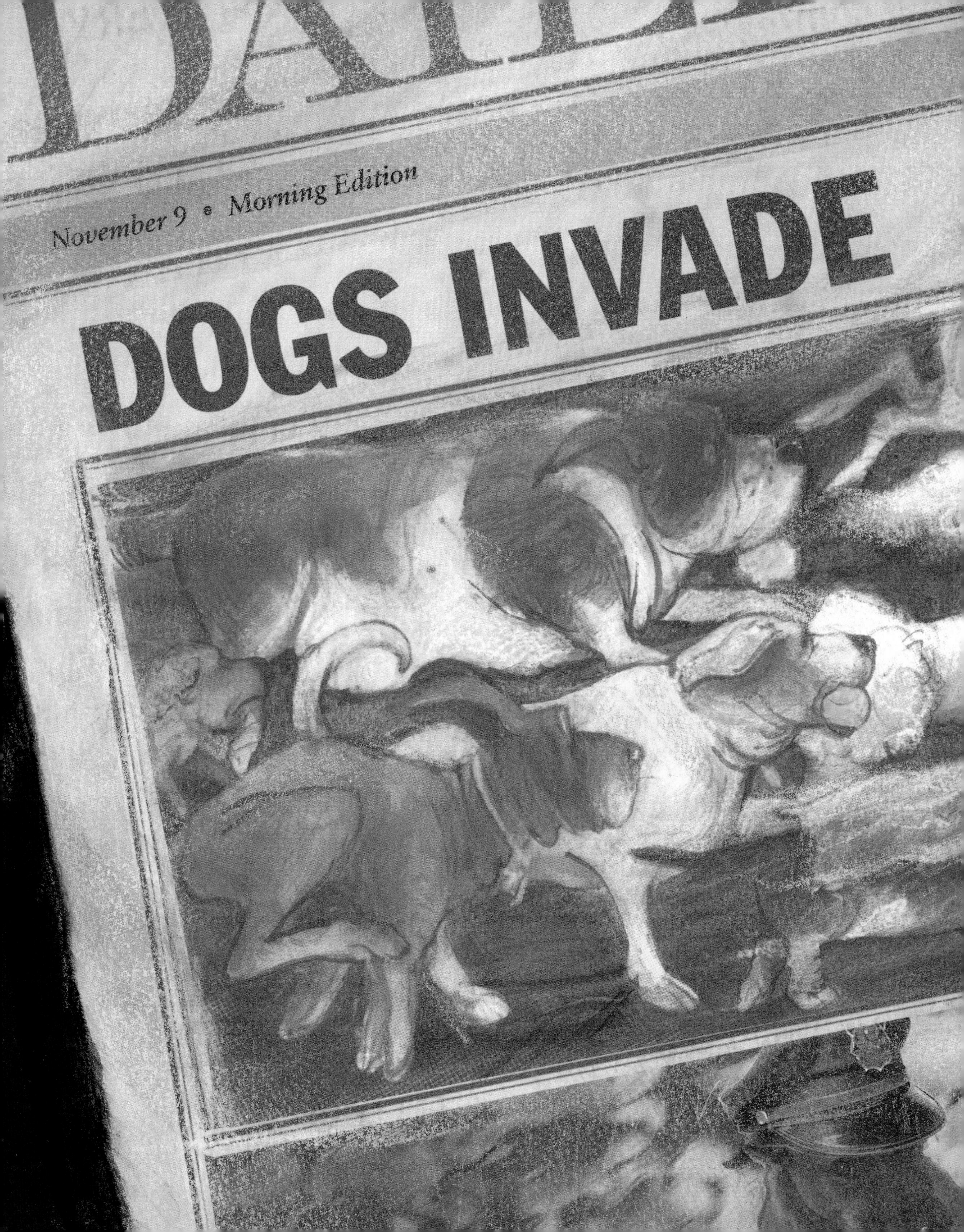
November 9 • Morning Edition
DOGS INVADE

# DOGWOOD!

One hundred and one dogs descended on the quiet town of Dogwood today, barking and racing willy-nilly through the streets. Who they are, why they are here, and where they are going remain unanswered questions as the investigation continues. "We are sniffing around," remarked Sheriff G. Shepherd. "We have some good leads, but are unable to comment at this time."

# CATastrophe!

One hundred and one dogs, believed to be the pack spotted earlier, departed Dogwood this afternoon in hot pursuit of a lone cat. The cat, identified as The Queen, resided at the house of the famous canine counselor, Mr. Mutt. "The dogs were apparently on a rescue mission," announced Sheriff G. Shepherd. "Mr. Mutt is safe. Case closed."

# MISSING CAT

Answers to the name The Queen.
Gray and white.
Last seen wearing tiara.
Cranky but loveable.
One of a kind.
Handle with care.
MR. MUTT MISSES HER.
(SORT OF.)

Please return ASAP to
100 Bonaparte Blvd.
Dogwood, DE 19091

**REWARD**

If the Couch Fits
Sleep on IT